g.n. hargreaves

douglas

EGMONT

Now, **this is a story about a dog.**
Not just any old, run-of-the-mill,
everyday, ordinary dog,
but an extraordinary dog.

A dog in a billion.

A dog called Douglas.

When other dogs chased balls, Douglas would sit inside
and sort through his stamp collection.

When other dogs lapped up water and chewed on a bone,
Douglas would sip tea and nibble cucumber sandwiches.

Douglas didn't go for walkies, he would sooner
go for a spin in his shiny red car.

And that's not all.

Douglas could play the tuba.

He could cycle up the tallest mountain
and he could ski down the steepest slope.

Douglas could do anything.

What a dog!

But, I'll let you into a little secret.
There was one thing he couldn't do.
One thing he desperately wanted to do.

He couldn't wag his tail.

You see to wag your tail, you need to know how to have fun.
But Douglas didn't know how to have fun.
Not at all. Not one bit.

Wherever he went people would laugh and jeer.

"What a bore!
What a drag!
He's no fun!
His tail won't wag!"

Poor Douglas. This made him feel glum. Very glum indeed.

One day, he began to cry. Two big, fat tears rolled down his cheeks and splashed on the ground. Plop! Plop!

"I wish I knew how to wag my tail," he sobbed.

Suddenly he heard a voice. A peculiar, squeaky sort of voice.

"Cheer up, fella," said a bird in a tree. "I'm Basil. Who are you?"

"Douglas," the gloomy dog sniffed.

"Here, borrow my hanky," said Basil, "and tell me why you're so down in the dumps."

Douglas told Basil all about his problems.

"That's serious," said Basil. "Never heard of a dog who couldn't wag his tail. We'll have to do something."

"But what?" asked Douglas.

"You could try having some fun," suggested Basil.
"Proper tail wagging, ball chasing, tummy tickling,
super smiley, giggly, wiggly, squiggly fun!"

So, Basil tried to persuade Douglas to chase a bouncy ball.

"Fetch!" cried Basil.

"I'd rather have a game of golf," replied Douglas.

Next Basil tried to take him for a walk. "Walkies!"

"Fiddlesticks! Where's the fun in that? I never walk anywhere."

"How about chasing cats?" asked Basil.

"Boring," said Douglas. "Let's play chess."

"You just don't know how to have fun," said Basil.

"But I can do everything else," boasted Douglas. "I can read, I can swim, I can ski. Why, I'm sure I could even fly if I put my mind to it."

"A FLYING DOG!" spluttered Basil. "Why, that's as ridiculous as a BARKING BIRD!"

"I don't see why," said Douglas. "Look, I can even beat you at chess. Checkmate!"

Basil thought about it for a moment.
And then he smiled.
And with a twinkle in his eye he said,
"Do you really think you could fly?"

"Of course," replied Douglas.

"Well, that might be fun. Certainly funny.
In which case, we'll have to find you a tree.
Somewhere high."

So they went in search of a tree. Not just any tree.
But the tallest tree in the wood.

"Now, that's what I call a whopper!" said Basil, pointing to a
huge tree that appeared to soar into the sky and touch the clouds.

Douglas began to climb up it.
He climbed and climbed. Up and up and up.
Higher and higher and higher.
And then he climbed some more.
Until, eventually, he reached the top.

Douglas crept along a branch and looked down at the tiny houses below. The fur on the back of his neck stood up. His heart went thud, thud, thud.

Douglas drew a deep breath, closed his eyes and took one giant step forward.

He flapped his paws up and down.

But nothing happened.

And then Doug*las fell.*

And he fell.

And then h*e fell some more.*

THUMP!

Douglas landed on a sheep,
and bounced,

BOING! into a big soft bush.

"Are you all right?" cried Basil.

"NO!" snapped Douglas, picking a twig from his fur.

"Your paws were flapping about all over the place,"
chuckled the bird.

"I suppose it was rather silly ..." said Douglas.

"SILLY!" hooted Basil. "It was ridiculously preposterous!"

And then, the most amazing thing happened ...

... Douglas smiled! And then the smile became a grin.
The grin became a chuckle. And the chuckle became a laugh.
A big, booming, hilarious HO HO, HA HA, HEE HEE!

Can you guess what happened next?

That's right ...

His tail began to wag!

"My, oh my," cheeped Basil. "Your tail's wagging!"

"Gosh!" Douglas laughed. "It does look funny!"

And that wasn't all ...

Douglas's tail started to wag faster …

And faster …

And faster still!

His tail was going so fast, it looked just like a speeding, whirling propeller.

And then suddenly … incredibly …
Douglas began to lift up into the air!

Up and up he went.

Higher and higher …

And higher still!

He looked around, and then down at the ground disappearing beneath him.

"Look! Look!" squawked Basil. "You're flying!
A flying dog, whoever heard of such a thing?
Why, that's as ridiculous as … as …"

"A barking bird?" suggested Douglas.

"WOOF! WOOF!"
said Basil.